Published in the UK by Scholastic, 2021
Euston House, 24 Eversholt Street, London, NW1 1DB
Scholastic Ireland, 89E Lagan Road, Dublin Industrial Estate,
Glasnevin, Dublin, D11 HP5F

SCHOLASTIC and associated logos are trademarks and/or
registered trademarks of Scholastic Inc.

Text © Chae Strathie, 2021
Illustrations © Nicola O'Byrne, 2021

The right of Chae Strathie and Nicola O'Byrne to be identified
as the author and illustrator of this work has been asserted by them
under the Copyright, Designs and Patents Act 1988.

ISBN 978 1407 19384 7
A CIP catalogue record for this book is available from the British Library.

Printed in Slovakia
Paper made from wood grown in sustainable forests and other controlled sources.

1 3 5 7 9 10 8 6 4 2

For amazing Albie, with
love and ROARS! xxx ~ C.S.

For Arabella, Natalie,
Cosmo, and Roxy ~ N.O.

DEAR
SPOOKYSAUR

Written by
Chae Strathie

Illustrated by
Nicola O'Byrne

SCHOLASTIC

Max was getting ready for Halloween.
He wanted to give everyone a big fright.

"Why don't you dress up
as a monster?" said Mum.

"Or a ghost?" said Dad.

But Max wasn't sure he'd be scary enough.

"I wish I was as fearsome as a DINOSAUR!" he said.

The next morning a letter arrived.
It was addressed to Max.

Dear Max,

As a Friend Of The Museum you are invited to a SPOOKTASTIC Halloween party in the Grand Hall.

Wear your creepiest costume to make this the scariest frightfest ever.

We look forward to seeing you for some MONSTROUS mayhem soon!

Yours scarily,

Dinosaur Dora

THE
CITY
MUSEUM
Natural History & Conservation

Max was so excited.

He loved the museum – especially the dinosaurs – and couldn't wait to tell his friend, T.Rex, that he'd be coming to see him soon. Max got out his paper and pencils and wrote a letter.

Dear T.Rex,

Have you heard there's going to be a Halloween party at the museum?

I've got the best idea for a costume, but I'm going to keep it secret so it's a BIG surprise.

What do dinosaurs do for Halloween? I bet you love it - you don't even have to dress up!

Yours excitedly,

Max

Max waited for T.Rex to reply.

He was helping make some spooky decorations when the letter arrived.

Dear Max,

ROOOOAAAARRRR!

It's so nice to hear from you.

What is this 'Halloween' thing? None of us dinosaurs have heard of it. Not even Troodon, and she's the smartest dinosaur there is. Halloween certainly wasn't around 65 million years ago when I lived outside.

Dinosaur Dora mentioned a party, but we're not allowed to go. For some reason she thinks people might be scared of us!

It's a shame because I LOVE a good party!

Yours sadly,

T.Rex

TOOT

Max was disappointed that T.Rex couldn't come,
but he had a brilliant idea to
cheer up his dinosaur friend . . .

Dear T.Rex,

I can't believe dinosaurs don't do Halloween
– you'd be GREAT at it!

Halloween is one night when people
dress up as anything they like.
Last year I was a bright green alien
and the year before I was a skeleton with
glow-in-the-dark bones.

I think you'll like my costume for the party.
The only thing is I might be too small
and not scary enough to make it work
– I'm definitely not as big and
fearsome as a dinosaur.

Yours worriedly,

Max

PS Why don't you have your own
dinosaur Halloween party?

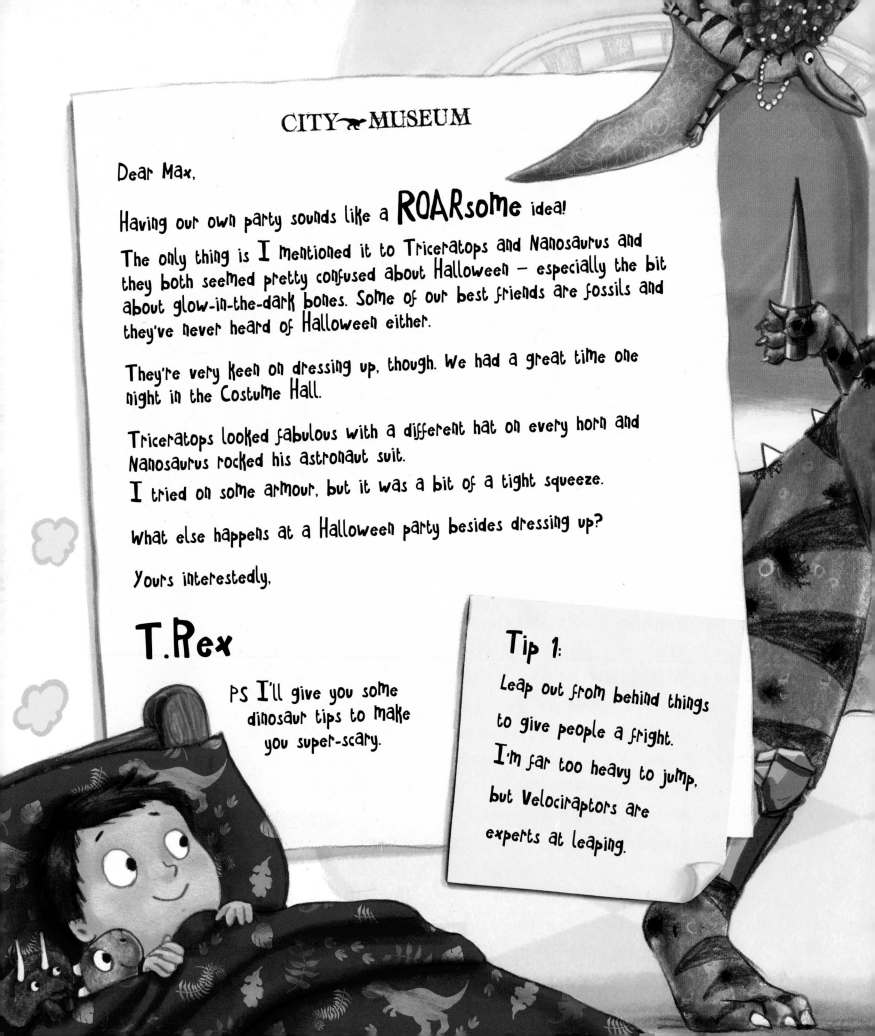

CITY ☭ MUSEUM

Dear Max,

Having our own party sounds like a **ROARsome** idea!

The only thing is I mentioned it to Triceratops and Nanosaurus and they both seemed pretty confused about Halloween — especially the bit about glow-in-the-dark bones. Some of our best friends are fossils and they've never heard of Halloween either.

They're very keen on dressing up, though. We had a great time one night in the Costume Hall.

Triceratops looked fabulous with a different hat on every horn and Nanosaurus rocked his astronaut suit.

I tried on some armour, but it was a bit of a tight squeeze.

What else happens at a Halloween party besides dressing up?

Yours interestedly,

T.Rex

PS I'll give you some dinosaur tips to make you super-scary.

Tip 1:

Leap out from behind things to give people a fright. I'm far too heavy to jump, but Velociraptors are experts at leaping.

Dear T.Rex,

I'm not making this up — Halloween parties are the
BEST!

As well as dressing up, people carve faces into pumpkins and decorate their houses. Then they tell jokes, sing songs or do dances and get lots of goodies. It's great!

Imagine a dinosaur-sized pumpkin. It would be as big as a car! Do you know any dinosaur jokes or can you boogie?

Yours dino-dancingly,

Max

PS Thanks for the tip. I leaped out at my sister, Millie, and she got a big fright, which was very funny. But I want to be even scarier. Do you have any other ideas?

CITY MUSEUM

Dear Max,

Hooray! The others have agreed to have a party! We can't wait to dress up.

I think I'll go as a bunny rabbit because my favourite toy is Pippin, which you gave me as a present when I got homesick on the dinosaur world tour.

Here's the invitation I made. What do you think?

I once made up a joke that goes:

Knock knock.
Who's there?

ROOOOOOOAAAAAAAAARRRRRRR!!!!!

People seem to find it more terrifying than funny, though. Perhaps you can help.

The last time I tried dancing I stood on Nanosaurus's toes then smashed two very expensive statues with my tail. Dinosaur Dora said it was the wrong kind of breakdancing.

Yours clumsily,

T.Rex

PS Try stomping. One of the heaviest dinosaurs ever was Argentinosaurus, which may have weighed as much as a blue whale. Imagine the thunderous thuds of its stomps!

COME TO THE
DINOSAUR PARTY
AND HAVE A FABULOUS TIME!

We're having Halloween
fun in the Dinosaur Hall
and YOU'RE invited!

So put on your **best** costume and join us
for singing, dancing, jokes and pumpkins.

HAPPY HALLOWEEN!

Max got the giggles when he read T.Rex's letter.
He could be a silly old dinosaur sometimes.

Dear T.Rex,

I love your drawings, but I should probably have mentioned that Halloween is supposed to be spooky rather than cute.

That means cobwebs, skeletons, spiders and bats — not fluffy bunnies!

I've made an invitation so you can see what I mean. Here's a dinosaur joke you can try:

What do you call a dinosaur that's fast asleep?

A DINO-SNORE!

Or how about this one?

What do you call a dinosaur that's covered in leaves and has a bird's nest on its head?

A TREE-REX!

Yours jokingly,

Max

PS I've tried stomping. Peanuts the cat thought it was pretty scary, but I think I can be much more fearsome.

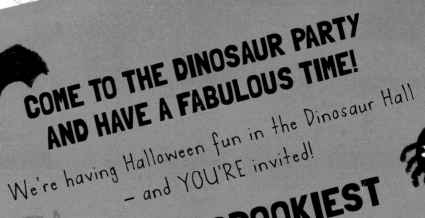

COME TO THE DINOSAUR PARTY AND HAVE A FABULOUS TIME!

We're having Halloween fun in the Dinosaur Hall — and YOU'RE invited!

So put on your **SPOOKIEST** costume and join us for singing, dancing, jokes and pumpkins.

HAPPY HALLOWEEN!

Max was putting the finishing touches to the Halloween decorations when the computer pinged.

It was an email addressed to him.

Send   Attach   Address   Fonts   Draft

From: T.Rex

Subject: Spooky

Dear Max,

I get it! 'Spooky' is the name of the game for the party tonight.

I'm getting the spiders from the Insect Hall to make cobwebs, the wolves are coming from the Animal Hall to do some howling, and the bats will be here too. I've even invited the mummies from the Ancient Egypt Hall. Those guys are super creepy!

We can't wait to dress up!
Have fun at your party tomorrow!

Yours Halloweenly,

T.Rex

PS The last thing to try is roaring. If you leap, stomp and roar you'll be sure to give everyone a HUGE Halloween fright!

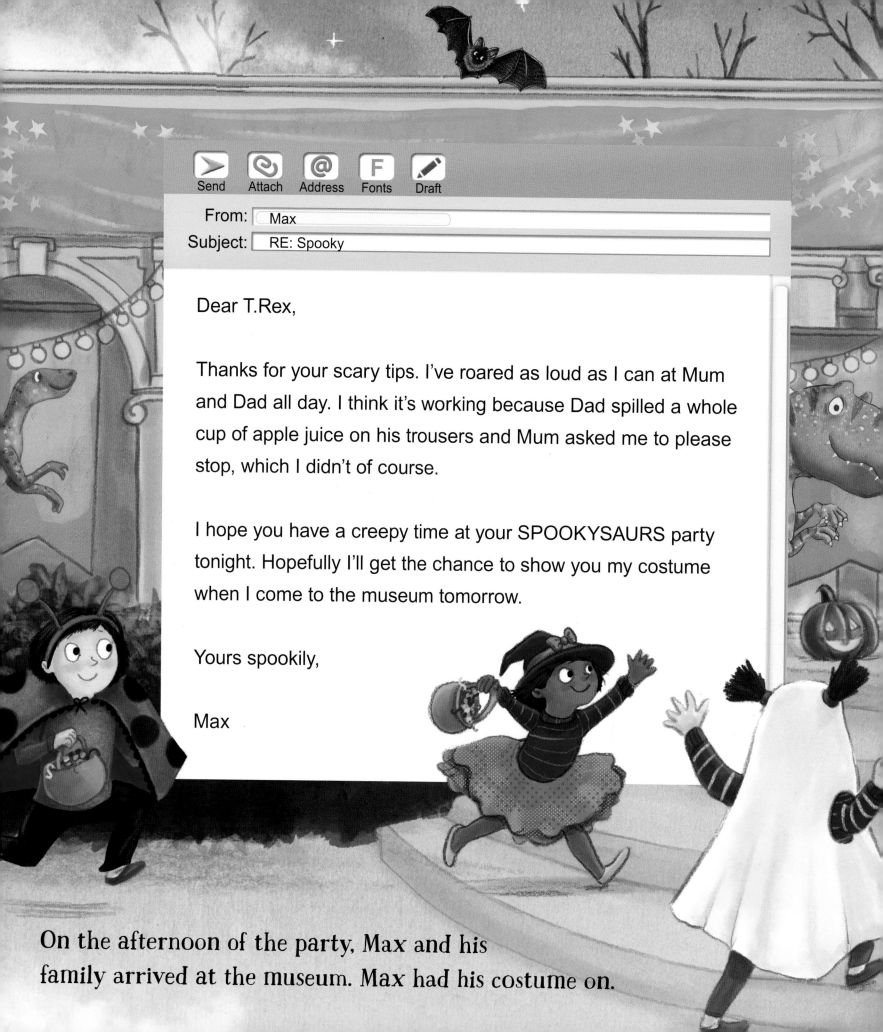

From: Max

Subject: RE: Spooky

Dear T.Rex,

Thanks for your scary tips. I've roared as loud as I can at Mum and Dad all day. I think it's working because Dad spilled a whole cup of apple juice on his trousers and Mum asked me to please stop, which I didn't of course.

I hope you have a creepy time at your SPOOKYSAURS party tonight. Hopefully I'll get the chance to show you my costume when I come to the museum tomorrow.

Yours spookily,

Max

On the afternoon of the party, Max and his family arrived at the museum. Max had his costume on.

"I'm a VAMPIRESAURUS!" he told Dinosaur Dora after he'd given her a fright with his jumping, stomping and roaring.

"You're VERY scary," said Dinosaur Dora.
"Now, I want to show you something rather odd."

She took Max into the Dinosaur Hall.

"It looks like someone's been having a
very spooky party in here," she said.

"The only thing is the T.Rex is
dressed as a bunny rabbit!"